DEDICATION

This book is both dedicated to the Spirit of all Native Peoples, past, present and future
as well as my children, grandchildren and great grand children. You all inspired me and gave
me the content to use for God our lord.

ACKNOWLEDGMENTS

I would like to acknowledge all the hard work that went into making this book a reality.
My late wife Sandy worked so hard to make this book happen, I love and miss you every day.
After her passing my daughter Erin and my Granddaughter Brittani whom
took over to keep my poetry alive.
I would not have been able to do it without my girls.

ISBN: 978-0692971932

This book belongs to:

The Adventures of Little Sparrow

LITTLE SPARROW'S FIRST HUNT

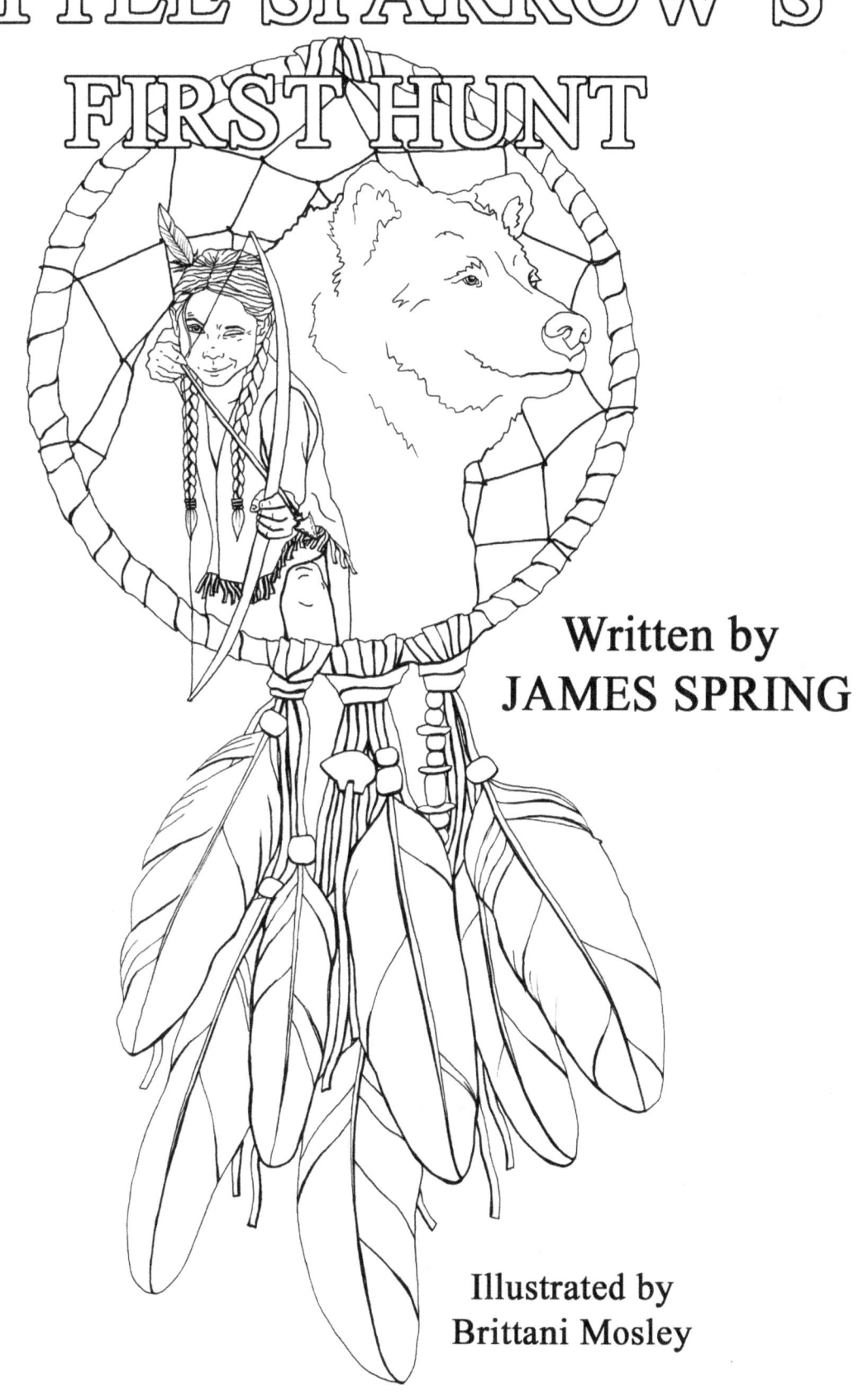

Written by
JAMES SPRING

Illustrated by
Brittani Mosley

Though he's only nine summers, Little Sparrow thinks the time is now,
To be a hunter and a warrior even if he knows not at all how.

He picks up his bow and arrows and heads to the forest deep,
Leaving in the early morning while his family is fast asleep.

He thinks they need some game upon which they can dine,

Certainly the meat of a rabbit or squirrel would be just fine.

As he moves deeper into the forest, he creeps quiet and slow,
The darkness is unnerving, he clutches tighter to his bow.

The boy warrior, at a sound freezes in fear,
For he sees the forest king, and already the bear is near.

He knows his tiny bow would barely make a scratch,
And his boyish strength against this giant certainly is no match.

It's no use to try to run, for he is merely but a child;
So small, alone and helpless facing a creature so strong and wild.

He moves through the trees and climbs on top of a rock
Never taking his eyes off the bear he watches him like a hawk.

Hoping to stand as if he's made of stone, so the bear will pass him by,
making him hidden and not a big bull's-eye.

His little heart beats faster when the bear picks up his scent,
Little sparrow watches the bear as his paws make dent by dent.

The trail led him straight his way
Little Sparrow is scared this is his last day.

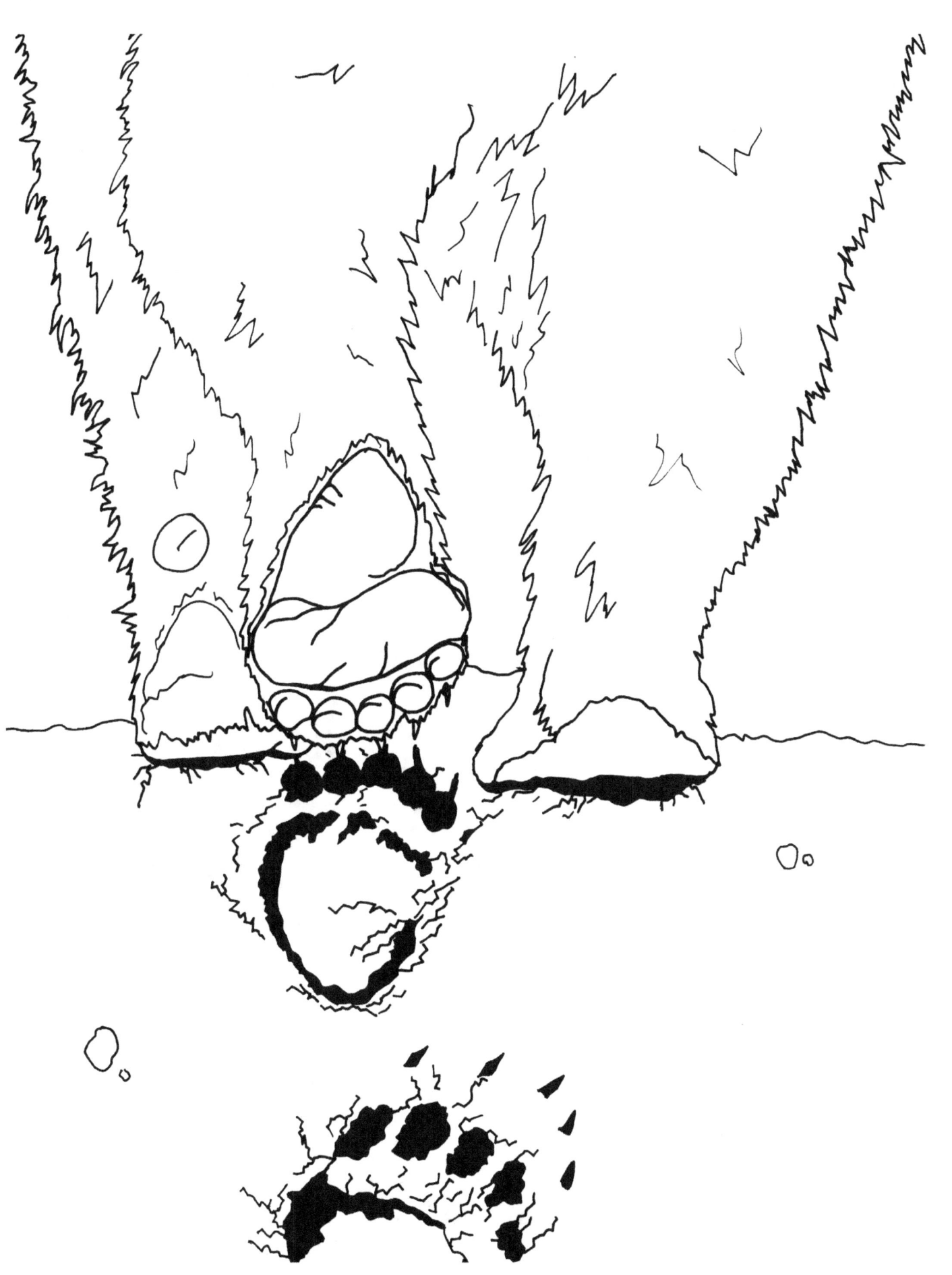

As the bear sniffs following Little Sparrow's trail, confused he seems to be,
He smells the aroma of a human, but a rock is what he sees.

The bear inhales even harder, his nose now but an inch away,
To the Great Spirit, the boy warrior begins to pray.

"Oh Great Spirit deliver me from this dreaded beast
I promise to thank you for not being the bear's next big feast."

The lungs of the mighty giant rocks the little boy,
They send his hair flying wildly as if he were a toy.

Little Sparrow wants to look, yet he's afraid of what he'll see,
He knows if the bear should want, he could swat him like a flea.

A rumbling moan vibrates the still forest air,
Though weary and shaken, he vows to escape the great bear.

As the wild thing sniffs the other way, the young warrior is relieved,
He smiles with happiness because he thinks the grizzly has been deceived

He hears the bear yawning and thinks "he's headed away",
But then is filled with fear when at his feet the bear decides to lay.

The bear leans against the rock on top of which Little Sparrow stands,
The beast is so mountainous, upon the boy's feet he also lands.

The little warrior tries to move, but his feet are held so tight,
He wiggles and squirms with all of his boyish might.

Unable to stand there until the bear's slumber is through.
Little Sparrow thinks hard about what he must do.

An idea comes to him, quick as a lightning flash:
Pull his feet out of his moccasins and then homeward he can dash!

He lifts one heel high to clear the soft tanned buckskin,
Then slowly extracts it from the trap it had been detained in.

He frees his other foot, giving thanks all the way home,
Thinking perhaps he's still too little for this big forest to roam.

THE
END

until the next
adventure

www.ingramcontent.com/pod-product-compliance
Lightning Source LLC
Chambersburg PA
CBHW081204170626
46813CB00009B/3318